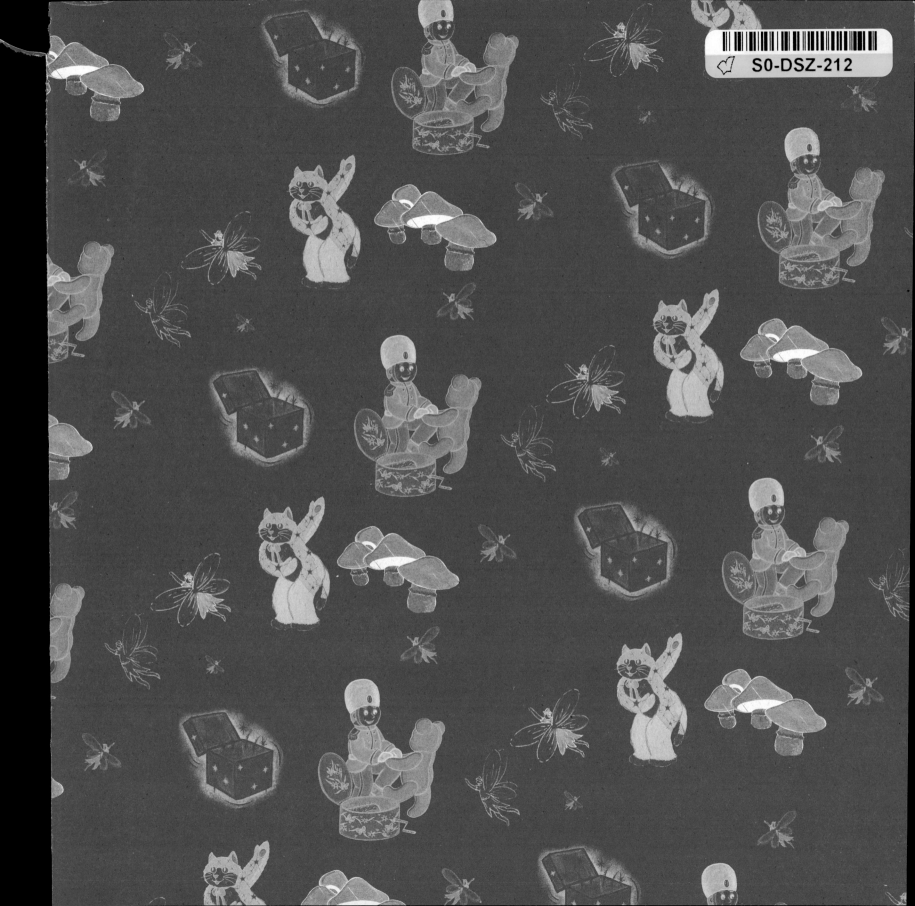

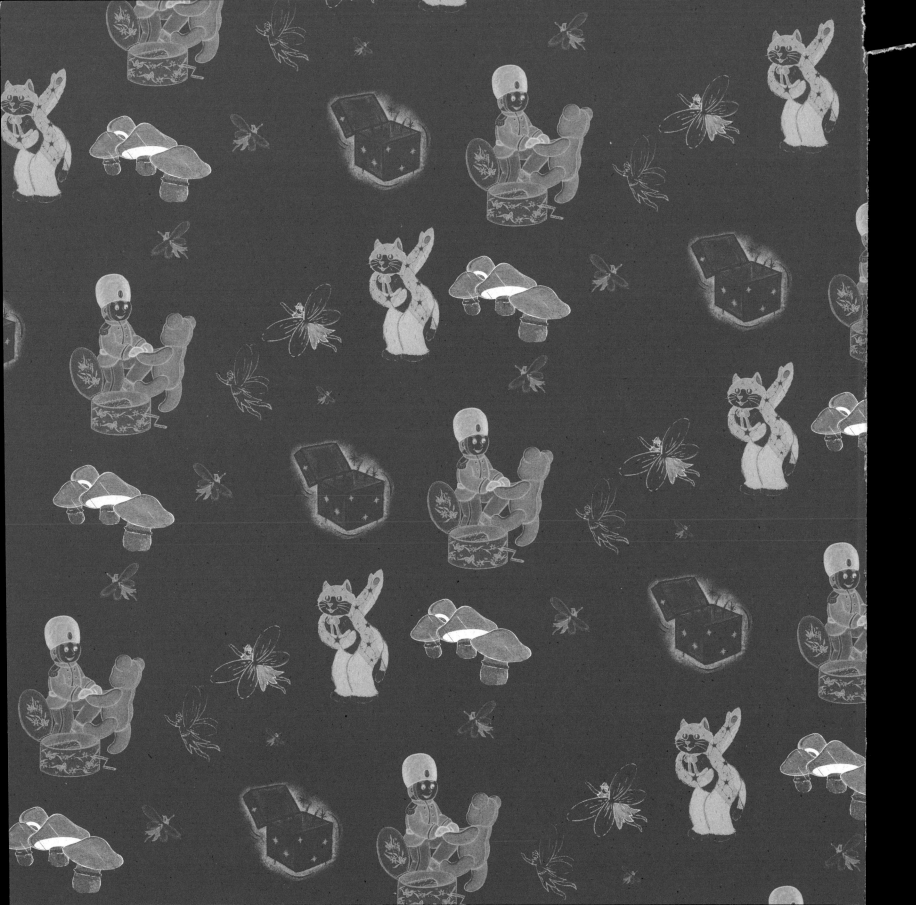

A Spell for a Puppy

~ & ~

Jinky's Joke

Published in 2003 by Mercury Books London
An imprint of the Caxton Publishing Group
20 Bloomsbury Street, London WC1B 3JH

© text copyright Enid Blyton Limited
© copyright original illustrations, Hodder and Stoughton Limited
© new illustrations 2003 Mercury Books London

Designed and produced for Mercury Books
by Open Door Limited
Langham, Rutland

Printed in China

Title: A Spell for a Puppy & Jinky's Joke
ISBN: 1 904668 23 2

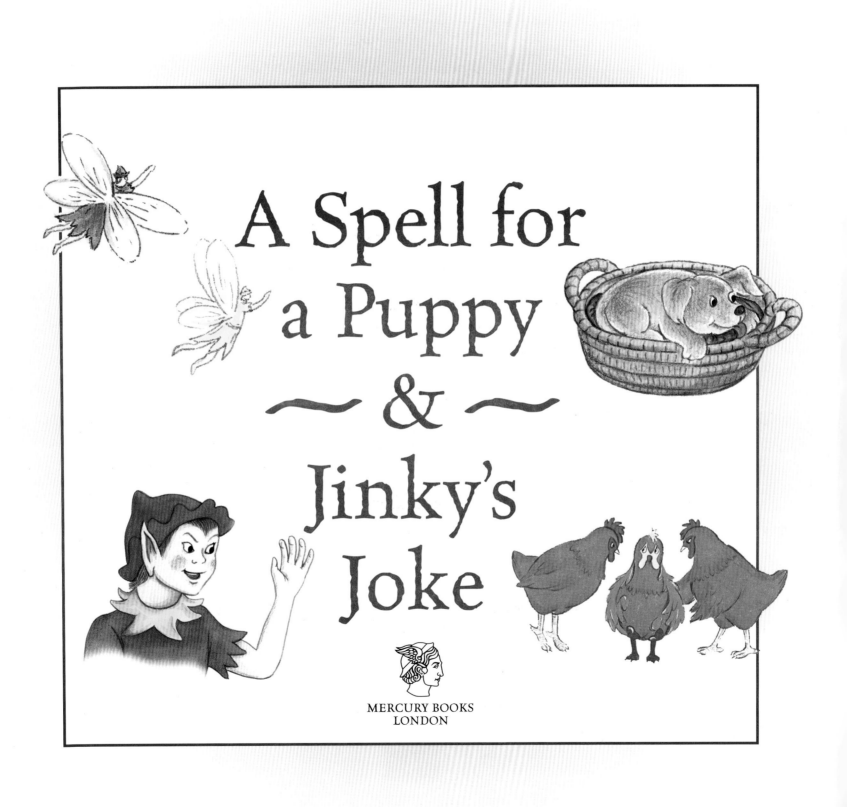

A Spell for a Puppy

~ & ~

Jinky's Joke

MERCURY BOOKS
LONDON

A Spell for a Puppy

There was once a little girl called Joan. She had a great many toys, books and games – almost every one you could think of. You might have thought she would be happy with so many, but she wasn't. She hadn't the one thing that she really did badly want – and that was a real, live puppy! Her mother didn't like dogs in the house, and would never let her have a puppy, or a kitten either.

"Why do you keep saying you want a puppy to play with?" she often said impatiently to Joan. "You have

so many lovely toys. What about your dolls' house? You never play with that now, Joan. Get it out this morning and give it a good clean. Take it out into the garden. It is nice and warm there, and it doesn't matter if you make a mess on the grass."

Joan didn't want to play with her dolls' house. She was not a little girl who was very fond of dolls. She liked running and jumping; she loved animals and birds. She wished she had been a boy. But she was obedient, so she fetched her dolls' house and took it out into the garden. She went down to the hedge at the bottom, where it was sheltered from the wind, for she did not want all the little carpets and curtains to blow away.

She took everything out and cleaned the house well with a wet cloth. She rubbed up the windows, and shook all the carpets. She polished the furniture and put it back again.

It was really a dear little house. There was a nice kitchen downstairs with a sink, and a fine drawing room and small dining room. Upstairs there was a little bathroom with a bath and a basin.

Three bedrooms opened out of one another, all papered differently, each with their little carpet on the floor.

"It's a pity, I don't like this sort of toy as most little girls do," thought Joan, as she arranged all the furniture. "I wish I did. But people like different things, I suppose – and I do love animals – and I do wish I had one of my very own."

Just then the dinner-bell rang, and Joan went off to wash her hands and brush her hair. She stood the little house under the hedge out of the sun. She meant to go back

after dinner and finish cleaning it outside. The front door knocker wanted a polish, and the chimney wanted washing.

But, after dinner, Mummy said she was going to take Joan out to tea, and the little girl was so pleased that she forgot all about the dolls' house out in the garden. She went off with her mother to catch the bus – and the little house was left under the hedge.

When Joan came back it was late and she was sent to bed at once. She snuggled down under the blankets – and then she suddenly remembered the dolls' house!

"Oh dear!" she said, sitting up in bed. "Whatever would Mummy say if she knew I had left my beautiful dolls' house out-of-doors? I really must go and get it!" She slipped on her dressing gown and went down the stairs. She went out of the garden door and ran down the path.

There was a bright
moon and she could
see everything quite
clearly. She went to
the hedge – and then
she stopped still in
the greatest surprise!

What do you think?
There were lights in her little dolls' house –
and people were walking about in the rooms
– and the front door was wide open!

"Whoever is in there?" thought Joan, in great excitement. She bent down to see – and to her great delight she saw that the little folk inside were pixies with tiny wings. They were running about, talking at the tops of their voices. They sounded like swallows twittering.

Joan looked into one of the bedrooms through the window – and she saw, fast asleep in one of the small beds, a tiny pixie baby. It was really too good to be true. The little girl sighed with delight – and the pixies heard her!

They slammed the front door at once – and one of them opened a bedroom window and looked out.

"Who are you?" they cried to Joan.

"I'm the little girl this house belongs to," said Joan. "I've been cleaning it to-day, and I left it here and forgot it. What are you doing here?"

"Oh, we found it and thought it would do so nicely for us and our family," said the pixie, in a disappointed voice. "You see, we lived in a nice hollow tree – but the woodmen came and cut it down – and we hadn't a home. Then we came along by your hedge and saw this lovely house. It's just the right size for us and, as there didn't seem to be anyone living in it, we thought we would take it."

"Well, I simply love to see you in it," said Joan. "I do really." "Would you let it to us?" asked the pixie. "We would pay you rent, if you liked."

"Oh, no," said Joan. "I don't want you to pay me for it. You can have it, if you like. I am very lucky to see you and talk to you, I think. I am most excited, really I am!"

"How kind of you to let us have it," said the pixie, beaming all over her little pointed face. "Can't we do something for you in return? Isn't there anything you want very much?"

"Well, yes, there is," said Joan. "I want a puppy dog very, very much. I have wanted one for years. But I have never had one."

"We'll give you a spell for one," said the pixie. She ran downstairs and opened the front door. She held up a very small box to Joan.

"Take this," she said. "There is a spell inside. Blow it out of your window to-night and say 'Puppy, puppy, come to me. Make me happy as can be. Puppy, puppy, come to me!'"

"Oh, thank you!" said Joan, more excited than ever. "Listen, pixie. Don't you think I'd better take your house to the woods to-morrow? The gardener often comes here and he might be cross if he saw I'd left my house in the hedge."

"Yes, that's a good idea," said the pixie.

"We would like to be somewhere in the woods. Will you carry the house there to-morrow morning? We'll show you where we'd like it."

"Yes, I will," promised Joan. "Now, I must go. Good night, and thank you very much."

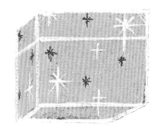

She ran off, looking back to see the little windows of her dolls' house lighted up so gaily. She went up to her bedroom and opened the small box. She took out the spell, which was like a tiny bit of thistledown, and blew it out of the window.

"Puppy, puppy, come to me. Make me happy as can be. Puppy, puppy, come to me!" she whispered.

Then she got into bed and fell fast asleep.

And whatever do you think happened next morning? Why, her Uncle Joe came to stay, and with him he brought a small, fat brown puppy in a basket – a present for Joan!

"Here you are!" he said to the delighted little girl. "I know you've always wanted a pup – and you shall have one! His name is Sandy – treat him well, and he'll be a good friend to you!"

Joan was full of joy. She loved the puppy, and it licked her nose and hands, pleased to have such a nice little mistress. She raced down the bottom of the garden with the puppy at her heels.

The dolls' house was still there, and outside stood all the pixies, waiting for her to come.

"I've got my puppy, I've got my puppy!" she said, joyfully. "The spell worked! Now, I'll carry your house to the woods!"

She picked it up and carried it off, the pixies half flying, half running in front to show her the way. She put it down in a little glade by the side of a small stream and said good-bye once more. Then she and Sandy raced home again, a very happy pair.

And if you should happen to come across a dolls' house in the woods, don't touch it, will you? It will be the one belonging to the pixies! They still live there, you see!

Jinky's Joke

Once there was a wicked little pixie called Jinky. He was always playing jokes on people, and sometimes they were funny, but more often they were not.

One week he went to all the shops that sold pails and saucepans and ordered dozens to be sent to old Dame Cooky. Well, the poor old lady couldn't imagine why so many saucepans and pails kept arriving, and she really grew quite frightened when she saw her kitchen piled up from floor to roof with them. It took her two whole days to take them back to the shops and explain that she hadn't ordered them.

Another time, Jinky put glue on the big wooden seat that stood outside the town hall. People sat there and waited for the bus. Oh dear, how angry everyone was when the bus came by and they got up – because they left half their skirts behind them!

Now one day Jinky found a few tins of paint as he passed the builder's yard. He tucked them under his arm with a grin. He meant to borrow some of that paint.

He stole into Mother Creaky's back-garden and called her hens to him. He painted those poor hens with the paint out of the tins till they looked like feathered rainbows!

"Oh, Henny-Penny, you do look queer!" said
Jinky, laughing as he set free a hen with a
red beak, a yellow comb, a purple tail, green
wings, and blue legs. And certainly the hen
did look very strange. All the other hens
looked at her, and then they ran at her and
began to peck her, for they
thought she was a stranger.

One by one, Jinky painted all the poor hens, and left them squabbling and pecking one another, for they couldn't bear to see such strange-looking creatures. Then Jinky heard Mother Creaky coming, and he hid behind the fence and watched.

"Oh! What's this I see?" cried Mother Creaky, in great astonishment, when she came to her gate. "Are these hens – or are they parrots or kingfishers? Never did I see such colours in my life!"

"Cluck, cluck, cluck!" said the hens sadly, and they ran to their mistress. They rubbed against her skirt and made it red, blue, green, orange, yellow, and purple.

"Oh, you poor creatures!" she cried. "Someone has painted you! You'll all have to be bathed."

Well, of course, hens hate the water, and Mother Creaky got pecked and scratched when she tried to get the paint off their feathers. She heard Jinky chuckling behind the fence, and caught sight of him running away. She was very angry.

"So that's Jinky again, is it?" she grumbled. "Well, it's time he got a fright. He left behind these paints – and I'll just go along to his house and do a little painting myself. I know he goes to supper with Higgle to-night. I shall have a nice time before he goes home."

So Mother Creaky picked up the tins of paint and went along to Jinky's cottage.

The front door was black, with a letterbox and a knocker above it.

Mother Creaky set to work.

She painted a big face! The letterbox was the mouth, and she painted that red. The knocker was the nose, and she painted that pink. She painted in big eyes and eyebrows and bright yellow hair and a witch's hat above it.

When she had finished, it looked exactly like a witch's face looking down the path. Mother Creaky laughed and hid behind a bush.

The night came and the moon shone out brightly. Jinky came home, whistling, laughing whenever he thought of Mother Creaky's hens.

He turned in at his gate – and then he saw the painted face looking at him from his front door!

"Owwwwww!" cried Jinky in fright. "Ooooooh! Owwwwww! What is it? What is it?"

Then Mother Creaky spoke in a deep voice from behind her bush. It seemed to poor Jinky as if the face on his door were speaking, and he listened in fright.

"Jinky!" said the deep voice. "How dare you play tricks on my friend, Mother Creaky! How dare you upset poor Dame Cooky! I have come to punish you!"

"Oh, please don't, please don't!" wept Jinky. "I won't play tricks again. I didn't know that Dame Cooky and Mother Creaky had a witch for a friend. Please forgive me."

"I will only forgive you if you promise not to play unkind tricks any more," answered the deep voice.

"I promise, I promise!" sobbed Jinky, trembling so much that he could hardly stand.

"Very well. You may come into your house and I will not harm you," said the voice. But Jinky didn't dare to go in. No – he turned and fled away. He spent the night most uncomfortably in a dry ditch, with beetles and spiders crawling all over him.

And in the morning when he crept back to his house, his front door was just the same as usual!

You see, Mother Creaky, with many giggles and chuckles, had washed away the witch's face with turpentine and water.

"He'll think twice before he plays a silly trick again," she said.

And Jinky did
think twice.
He didn't tell
a single person
about the witch
he had seen –
but Dame Creaky
told the ice-cream
man, and he
told me – so
that's how I know!

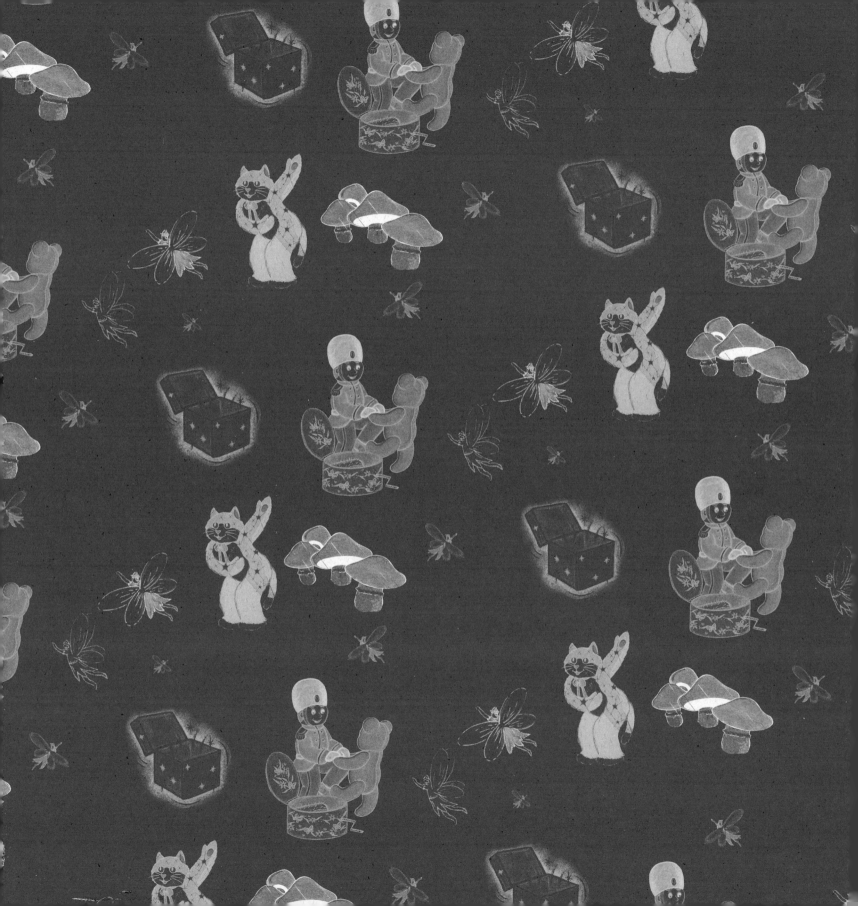